Ellie the Homesick Puppy

Other titles by Holly Webb

The Snow Bear

The Reindeer Girl

The Winter Wolf

Animal Stories:

Lost in the Snow

Alfie all Alone

Lost in the Storm

Sam the Stolen Puppy

Max the Missing Puppy

Sky the Unwanted Kitten

Timmy in Trouble

Ginger the Stray Kitten

Harry the Homeless Puppy

Buttons the Runaway Puppy

Alone in the Night

Jess the Lonely Puppy

Misty the Abandoned Kitten

Oscar's Lonely Christmas

Lucy the Poorly Puppy

Smudge the Stolen Kitten

The Rescued Puppy

The Kitten Nobody Wanted

The Lost Puppy

The Frightened Kitten

The Secret Puppy

The Abandoned Puppy

The Missing Kitten

The Puppy Who was Left Behind

The Kidnapped Kitten

The Scruffy Puppy

The Brave Kitten

The Forgotten Puppy

The Secret Kitten

A Home for Molly

My Naughty Little Puppy:

A Home for Rascal

New Tricks for Rascal

Playtime for Rascal

Rascal's Sleepover Fun

Rascal's Seaside Adventure

Rascal's Festive Fun

Rascal the Star

Rascal and the Wedding

Ellie the Homesick Puppy

Holly Webb

Illustrated by Sophy Williams

For Tom, Robin and William

www.hollywebbanimalstories.com

STRIPES PUBLISHING
An imprint of Little Tiger Press
1 The Coda Centre, 189 Munster Road,
London SW6 6AW

A paperback original
First published in Great Britain in 2010

Text copyright © Holly Webb, 2010
Illustrations copyright © Sophy Williams, 2010
Author photograph copyright © Nigel Bird
My Naughty Little Puppy illustration copyright © Kate Pankhurst

ISBN: 978-1-84715-113-1

A CIP catalogue record for this book is available
from the British Library.

Printed and bound in China.

10 9 8

Chapter One

"Megan, you're meant to be packing those books, not reading them!"

Megan looked up guiltily at her mum.

"Sorry! I found this one down the side of my bed, and I'd forgotten I'd even got it. I haven't read it for ages." Megan reluctantly put the book inside a box and sighed.

Mum smiled. "Oh, go on, you can keep it out – we've got a couple more days till we go anyway. You'll go mad without a book to read."

Megan nodded and laid the book on her pillow as Mum headed back downstairs. She sat down on her bed and shook her head disbelievingly.

"A couple more days, Ellie. Only two more nights sleeping in this bedroom," she murmured.

Ellie clambered up on to Megan's knee, wagging her tail, and then licked her hand lovingly. She didn't know why Megan sounded worried, but she wanted to help.

"You're excited too, aren't you?" Megan said, smiling. "You haven't got to go to a new school though, lucky Ellie."

She stroked Ellie's golden ears, and the little puppy shivered with delight. Then she curled up on the duvet again, working herself into a little yellow furry ball.

Moving house was exciting and scary at the same time. Megan's bedroom in the new house was much bigger than this one, which would be great – but then she was really going to miss her best friend Bella, and all her mates from school. They had broken up for the Easter holidays the day before, and everyone in her class had got together to make her a huge card, with all their photos on it and a message from each of them. She'd almost cried when they gave it to her, thinking how they'd all tried so hard to make it special. It was sitting on her desk now, so she could pack it very carefully at the top of one of the boxes, last thing. Megan looked at it and sighed.

It wasn't as if they were actually

moving all that far – only about ten miles; it wasn't the other side of the country, or anything like that. But it meant a new school, of course, and a whole load of new people. *New friends*, Megan told herself firmly.

The best thing was that in two days' time, Megan and Ellie would be able to step out of their back door and ramble wherever they wanted. Here they only had the park, and Megan wasn't allowed to walk Ellie on her own. She knew she was going to have to be very careful going for walks in the countryside near their new house, and every time she mentioned it, Mum kept reminding her about being responsible and not going too far. But all the same, she was practically going to have a wood at the end of her garden! It was going to be brilliant! She'd be able to take Ellie over to her gran's house, too, as Gran lived just about in walking distance from their new house.

Megan gently stroked Ellie's soft golden back, and the little dog gave a sleepy whine and half rolled over, inviting Megan to stroke her tummy. She yawned hugely, showing her very white teeth, and opened her eyes, blinking lovingly up at Megan.

Megan smiled back at her. "I just can't wait to take you for walks in those woods," she whispered happily. "It's going to be the best thing ever!"

Ellie sprang up and gave an excited, hopeful little bark.

Megan laughed. "You heard me say

the W word, didn't you, Ellie-pie? I can't believe you want to go out again, we've only been back home an hour!"

Ellie was wagging her tail madly now, staring up at Megan, but Megan shook her head.

"I'm sorry, Ellie. Mum says I have to pack."

Ellie didn't understand exactly what Megan was saying, but she knew what that tone of voice meant. No walk. She lay back down on the bed, her head resting mournfully on her paws. She knew they'd had a long walk, but now she'd had a little sleep, she felt just like another run.

Megan laughed at her. "You're such an actress, Ellie! You're behaving like I never take you for walks. And it's not fair, because you know I'd love to. But we have to get everything into boxes." She sighed. "And Mum's only given me these ones. She says if I can't get all my stuff in here, I'm going to have to sort some of it out and get rid of it." She looked round her room worriedly. It seemed an awful lot to fit into such a small stack of boxes.

Megan went over to the window sill and started to pack her collection of toy dogs into a box. She had loads, all different breeds, but more than half of them were Labradors, like Ellie. Officially, she was a Yellow Labrador, but Megan thought yellow wasn't the right word at all. Ellie was really a rich honey-golden colour, with pale cream fur on her tummy. Her ears were a shade darker than everywhere else, and super-silky. Mum reckoned that Ellie might get darker as she got older, to match her ears, but Megan wasn't sure. She would be growing for ages, anyway; she was just four months old at the moment. But even though Ellie was only a puppy, she was always bursting with energy.

Ellie stared soulfully at Megan, watching her tape up the box. It looked fun. Her ears twitched, and her tail wagged a little. Perhaps she could jump at that tape? She was never quite sure what was naughty, and sometimes jumping at things got her told off…

Suddenly, Ellie's ears pricked up. She could hear someone coming down the path. Tail wagging, she stood up on the bed to look out of the window, and gave Megan a little warning bark. It was Bella!

Before Bella even had the chance to ring the bell, Megan and Ellie raced out of the room and down the stairs, making for the front door. Ellie won easily. She always did. She was amazingly fast. She scrabbled at the front door with her paws, barking excitedly, until Megan caught up.

"Ssshh! Ellie, ssshh! Come back, look, I can't open the door when you've got your paws on it, can I?"

Ellie scampered back, panting excitedly. She knew Megan's friend Bella, and she hoped this meant a walk after all. She was used to walking with Bella, as Megan and her mum usually picked Bella up on the way to school. Ellie and Megan often walked round the corner to Bella's house when they went to the park too, as Megan's parents didn't like her going on her own, even when she had Ellie with her.

"Hi, Megan! Mum said I could come round and help you pack, if that's OK with your mum and dad?" Bella looked hopefully at Megan's dad, who was struggling into the hall carrying a massive box of china from the kitchen.

"Umph! Fine by me," Dad said, putting down the box carefully. "But make sure you *do* pack, girls, OK? Not just chatting."

Bella stared around Megan's room. "All these boxes!" She slumped down on Megan's bed sadly, and Ellie scrambled up after her to lick her face. "Oof, not so much, Ellie! Oh, Megan, I've known for ages you were going, but it seems so real now."

Megan sat down beside her, and Ellie wriggled happily between them. "I know. Packing makes it seem as though it really is happening. The day after tomorrow..." Megan's voice wobbled, and Ellie turned to lick her too. What was the matter with them both? She looked worriedly from Megan to Bella and back again, making her big puppy ears swing. Something was definitely wrong. Ellie stood up with her paws on Megan's shoulder, and stuffed her cold black nose firmly into Megan's ear. That always made her laugh.

Megan did laugh this time too, and so did Bella, but somehow they still sounded sad.

"I suppose at least we can send each other emails," Bella said, reaching out to stroke Ellie, and Megan nodded.

"And we can phone." Megan laughed. "Mum said she thought they might have to get me my own phone line, or they'd never get to use the phone themselves! It won't be the same as taking Ellie to the park with you, though."

Ellie stood on the bed, listening to them with her head on one side. Something was definitely going on.

"I'm going to miss her too," Bella agreed, tickling Ellie's ears. "You know Mum still won't let me get a dog because she says we haven't got the time to look after one. Now I won't even be able to share Ellie with you. And she's growing so quickly. I probably won't recognize her soon."

Ellie wagged her tail delightedly

as Bella fussed over her.

"I'll email you loads of photos," Megan promised. "And you're coming to stay. Mum and Dad are going to get me a sleepover bed that slides under mine. Ellie can be half your dog again then."

"You'd better record her bark for me, too," Bella reminded her. "I'll never get out of the house for school in the morning without Ellie barking outside the gate."

Ellie yawned. Megan and Bella kept fiddling around with those boxes and talking, and no one was taking her for a walk. She was bored. She slid off the bed and squeezed underneath it. There were always interesting things to play with under there…

"I knew it!" Megan's dad put his head round the door five minutes later. "You two are sitting there chatting, instead of filling boxes."

"Sorry!" Megan and Bella jumped up, and Megan grabbed a pair of trainers and stuffed them quickly into a box, just to look busy.

"And what's Ellie doing under there?" Dad asked, peering round the end of Megan's bed.

Ellie crept out from under the bed looking rather guilty, with half a roll of brown packing tape attached to her whiskers. It was very chewy, though she didn't really like the taste, and it seemed to have stuck...

"Naughty Ellie!" Megan giggled. "Sorry, Dad. I'll clean her up…"

Dad shook his head. "Honestly, after she ate your mum's shoe yesterday, you'd think she'd have had enough of chewing things. Just keep an eye on her, OK?"

Megan nodded apologetically, and started to peel the tape off Ellie's muzzle. "Silly dog," she muttered lovingly, as Ellie squirmed. "Yes, I know it's not nice, but you can't go round with parcel tape all over you. There!"

After that the girls made a real effort to get on with packing, and for the next hour they hardly even chatted at all.

Ellie whined miserably. After Megan had taken the tape away and told her off, she'd sat so patiently, waiting for someone to play with her, or take her for a walk, or at least stroke her. But Megan and Bella just kept taking things off the shelves and putting them into those strange-smelling boxes. Ellie didn't like it. This was her room, and it was changing. She liked it the way it was before.

"Oh, Ellie, are you bored?" Megan picked her up, hugging her gently. "I wish I could play with you too. But we won't be much longer."

"Actually, I told Mum I'd be back around now," said Bella, hugging Megan and Ellie both at the same time. "I can't believe you've only got tomorrow left!" She gulped. "I wish Mum hadn't arranged for us to go and see my cousins, not on your last day. Call me soon? Promise! Bye, Megan!" Then she dashed out of the room and down the stairs, almost slamming the front door behind her.

Megan sat down limply on her bed, looking round at the piles of boxes, all labelled by Bella in her favourite glittery felt tips with her best spelling, which was dreadful. "It's going to be brilliant," she told Ellie again, but this time she didn't feel quite so sure.

Chapter Two

Packing up had been an adventure to start with, but by the second day, everyone was starting to get grumpy. It was such a huge job. The removals van was coming early the next morning, and everything had to be packed up by then. Megan could tell that her mum was panicking that they wouldn't be ready in time.

She was trying to stay out of the way as much as possible, but it wasn't easy with Ellie. Mum and Dad were far too busy to take her for a proper walk, and Megan wasn't allowed to go out on her own, so Ellie was full of energy, and she couldn't work it off properly. Already that morning she'd chewed a roll of bubble wrap into tiny pieces all over the living room floor, and she kept managing to be in everyone's way.

"Mum, stop!" Megan yelled, as her mum lowered a box of books on to the hall floor.

"What? What is it?" Her mum straightened up, red-faced with effort, and peered worriedly over the top of the huge box.

"You were just about to squish Ellie with that!" Megan helped her mum put the box down on top of another one, then pointed to the space she'd been aiming for. Ellie was sitting there, wagging her tail and looking very pleased with herself.

Mum sighed. "You're going to have to take her into the garden. I'm sorry, Megan, but Ellie's going to get hurt in a minute. She's better off outside."

"Come on, Ellie!" Megan tried to sound enthusiastic as she led Ellie out into the garden. She'd found the red-and-white-striped knotted rope toy that Bella had given Ellie for Christmas in her basket, so at least they could play.

Ellie loved racing up and down the garden after the rope, it was her favourite toy, although she didn't see why she always had to give it back to Megan after she'd fetched it. It was much more fun to chew it to bits. She shook her head vigorously as Megan tugged at the toy, laughing.

"Give it here, you silly girl! I'm going to throw it again!"

"Megan, can you come here a moment!" It was Mum, calling from inside. With everyone already a bit grumpy, she knew she'd better go and see what Mum wanted, rather than pretend she hadn't heard.

"I'll be back in a minute," she promised Ellie, and dashed inside.

Ellie shook the toy a few more times and growled at it, in case it was thinking of fighting back. At last she dropped it on the grass, nosing it hopefully. Where was Megan? This game wasn't as much fun without her. Ellie left the toy and trotted up the garden to the back door.

The door was closed, but Ellie scrambled up the back step, anyway. The door didn't always shut properly, and sometimes she could open it, if she nudged it hard with her nose at just the right place. Ellie pushed at the door. She wagged her tail proudly as it swung open and trotted inside.

Ellie wandered along the hallway, listening for Megan. Ah! That was her voice, coming from upstairs. She bounded up the stairs to find her.

Unfortunately, Megan's dad was coming down the stairs, with his arms full of pictures from the bedrooms that he needed to bubble-wrap.

Ellie yowled as he accidentally trod on her paw, and tried to shoot off through his legs.

Megan's dad stumbled down the stairs, twisting his ankle. He landed painfully at the bottom.

Clutching his ankle, he looked up to see Ellie staring down at him.

"That stupid dog!" he yelled. "Megan! Ellie just tripped me up on the stairs. You're supposed to be watching her! I thought Mum told you to put her outside."

Megan and her mum had heard the crash, and they were already running along the landing.

"She didn't mean to!" Megan protested, hurrying to pick up Ellie, who was whimpering in fright. "I'm sorry, Dad, she *was* outside. I can't have shut the back door properly – it wasn't her fault. Are you OK?"

"No," her father muttered crossly, stretching his ankle. "Take that dog outside, now. Ow!"

Megan carried Ellie back into the garden. The little dog was shivering. She wasn't used to being shouted at, and she'd never heard Megan's dad sound so cross. Megan sat down on the garden bench and cuddled Ellie, whispering soothing words. "Ssshh, he didn't mean it. I'm sorry, Ellie, I should have made sure you couldn't get back in."

Ellie snuggled into her fleecy top, still shaking. At least Megan wasn't angry with her. She whined with pleasure as Megan stroked her ears.

She knew Megan would always be there to look after her.

Chapter Three

Ellie rested her chin on Megan's shoulder, as she lovingly stroked her head over and over.

"Megan!" Mum was calling from inside. Megan stood up slowly, carrying Ellie. She was growing so fast! She had been so small when they got her, it had been easy to hold her like this. But now she was getting to be a real weight.

"Oof, Ellie, my arms are going to fall off," Megan teased her lovingly, as she carried her up the garden. She felt Ellie tense up a little as they went into the kitchen to join Mum and Dad. Obviously she remembered Dad shouting at her. "Hey, ssshhh, it's OK," she whispered. But Ellie buried her nose in Megan's neck and whimpered.

"Is Ellie all right?" Mum asked. "She didn't get hurt too, did she?"

Megan shook her head. "No, I think she's just a bit upset. She didn't know what was going on. I'm really sorry she tripped you up, Dad. How's your ankle?"

Dad had it propped up on the chair in front of him, covered by a bag of frozen peas. "I'll live. But this has made us think, Megan. Mum and I have talked it over, and we're sure it's the right thing to do now…"

"What is?" Megan asked cautiously. From the way Mum and Dad were looking, she had a feeling it was going to be something she wouldn't like.

"Ellie's really been getting in the way while we've been packing, Megan," Mum explained. "It's going to be the same when the removal men are loading up, and when we're unpacking at the new house, too. It's just not practical having a puppy around. Dad could have been hurt really badly."

"She didn't mean to," Megan pleaded. "She's only little. She wasn't trying to be naughty."

"We know that, but we're so busy, and no one has the time to exercise Ellie properly right now. So she's even bouncier and sillier than usual! Aren't you, hey?" Dad reached out very gently to stroke the puppy. "Oh dear, I really did frighten her," he said sadly, as he saw Ellie's eyes widen nervously as he came close. "It isn't fair on her."

Megan gulped. She could see that they were right – she could hardly argue that Ellie wasn't getting in the way, when Dad was sitting there with a hurt ankle. "But, what are you going to do?" she whispered. "You're not going to make us give her back to Mrs Johnston, are you?" Mrs Johnston was the breeder who had sold Ellie to them. She felt tears starting to well up in her eyes. "Please don't say we have to give her back!" she choked out. "It wasn't her fault, I'll be more careful, I promise!"

"Megan, Megan, calm down! Of course we're not sending Ellie back."

Mum laughed, hugging her and Ellie. "This is only for a few days while we move. We don't want to get rid of Ellie, but when we first started planning the move, your gran said she could help out and have Ellie for a bit if we needed her to. So I rang Gran just now, and she said she'd love to have her. She'll drive up and get Ellie, and take her back to Woodlands Cottage until we've settled in a bit, just for a couple of days. We'll pick her up on Tuesday."

"We're all going to be so busy, you'll hardly notice she's gone," Dad said encouragingly.

Megan held Ellie tightly, feeling the warm weight in her arms. She didn't want to send Ellie away. Not when she was already upset. She was sure Ellie would hate it.

"She won't understand," she said sadly. "I know she loves Gran, but she's never stayed with her. She's never stayed anywhere without me! She'll think I've abandoned her... She's really confused with all the packing already, and she doesn't understand what's going on. Couldn't I just be really, really careful and keep her in the garden and not let her get in the way?" Megan begged. "I know Gran will look after her, but Ellie's used to having me. She'll be miserable somewhere else. And Gran's got a cat – that's not going to work! Sid will hate having Ellie in the house!"

Megan looked down at the puppy. Ellie quite liked chasing cats...

"I'm sure your gran will sort them out," Dad said, smiling. "Sid and Ellie will probably be curled up on the sofa together by the time we go and pick Ellie up."

Megan shook her head disbelievingly. "Please…?" she whispered.

Mum sighed. "I'm sorry, Megan. We've already had one accident. And I nearly squashed Ellie with that box this morning. This just isn't the right place for a puppy right now. And the new house, too. We don't really know what it's like – there might be all sorts of places where she could get herself into trouble. We need to check everything out first to make sure she's safe."

Ellie gave an anxious little whine. She could feel that Megan wasn't happy, and she didn't like it. She licked Megan's cheek lovingly and looked at her with big, worried eyes.

Megan pressed her cheek gently against Ellie's soft ears. It wasn't just Ellie who was going to hate this. Megan had been counting on having Ellie to cheer her up over the next couple of days. It was going to be so hard to leave her old home and her best friend. And now it looked like she was going to have to do it all on her own.

Gran drove up from Westbury later that afternoon to pick Ellie up. Ellie had a special dog cage for travelling, and it just about fitted on the back seat of Gran's car. Megan carefully packed up Ellie's basket and blanket, and her bowls and food – including her favourite bone-shaped biscuits. Then there was a bagful of toys, her lead, her blanket – the list went on and on.

"Goodness," Gran murmured. "How many dogs am I looking after?"

"Thanks so much for doing this," said Megan's mum. "It's a huge help."

Ellie was trotting backwards and forwards after Megan as she carried all her things to make a pile in the hall. She was very confused about what was going on, but she'd seen Megan's dad moving her travel cage into Gran's car, so she thought she and Megan must be going somewhere with Gran. They had driven out for special walks in the woods with her before. It must be that. Though Ellie didn't see why she would need her basket and everything else just to go out for the day.

"Right." Gran finished her cup of tea. "We'd better be off then, if we don't want to get back too late. We'll see you all on Tuesday." She hugged Megan. "Oh, I'm so excited about having you all living so close. It's going to be lovely."

Megan hugged her back. She was excited too, but she couldn't help worrying about Ellie. "Gran, you will make sure she's not lonely tonight, won't you? She usually sleeps on my bed," she reminded her anxiously.

"I'll do my best," Gran promised. "I think Sid would leave home if a dog came and tried to sleep on my bed with him, but how about I give Ellie a hot water bottle?"

Megan nodded sadly, as she pictured Ellie spending the night on her own.

"It's only for two days, Megan,"

Dad said, putting an arm around her shoulders. "Ellie will be fine."

Ellie hopped into her cage happily enough, expecting Megan to come and sit next to her on the back seat. She would probably waggle her fingers through the door and tickle her ears.

But Gran was getting into the car without Megan. Ellie looked around anxiously, and barked to tell her she'd made a mistake. Gran looked back over her shoulder, and smiled. "It's all right, Ellie. Shh-shh. Don't worry, we'll see Megan again soon."

Ellie stared back at her. Yes, *Megan*. Gran must know what was wrong. Why were they going without Megan? She felt the vibrations as Gran started the car and howled in despair. Megan was being left behind! Ellie stood up on her hind legs in the cage, trying to look out of the window, but she could only see the side of the car and Gran's seat in front.

Megan was clinging to her mum's arm, trying to stop herself racing after Ellie and yelling at Gran to stop the car. "Oh, Mum, listen to her howling," she said miserably. "She's so upset. Does she really have to go to Gran's?"

Her mum just hugged her.

Ellie couldn't see Megan, but she could hear her, and she sounded unhappy. She scrabbled frantically at the bars of her cage with her paws, desperate to get back to Megan.

As the car pulled away down the road, Ellie barked and barked.

At last, when it hurt to bark any

more, she stopped. She pressed her nose against the door of the travel cage.

Gran had taken her away from Megan, and Megan hadn't wanted her to go. Of course she hadn't! Ellie was Megan's dog. Ellie didn't understand what was going on, but she was absolutely certain about one thing.

She had to get back to Megan.

At Gran's house, everything smelled different. Ellie had been there before, but only with Megan, when it had been fun. Gran was doing her best – she'd taken Ellie for a walk when they first arrived, to stretch her legs after being shut up in the car. But Ellie had trailed along behind her with her ears drooping, and in the end Gran had turned back.

But it was worse in the house. Ellie didn't want to be here, and she *hated* cats. Sid was huge and black and old, and very grumpy. He didn't like dogs at all, and he really didn't like dogs who barked and jumped around all over the place. He stood on the back of an armchair and hissed angrily when he first saw Ellie. With all his fur standing up like that and his tail fluffed up like a brush, Sid was nearly as big as she was.

Gran carefully made sure they were kept apart after that, shutting Ellie in the kitchen. But then the phone rang, and she forgot to close the kitchen door when she came out to the hall to answer it. Ellie trotted out after her – she might not want to be here, but Gran was her one link with Megan.

Sid was sitting in the middle of the hallway like a furry black rock.

Ellie bounced at him bravely and barked, but Sid shot forwards and scraped his claws across her nose. Ellie yelped. She'd chased cats before, or tried to anyway – Megan didn't like her chasing things. But the cats had never fought back before. She stared at Sid worriedly, and he hissed again. It was a clear warning.

Ellie crept behind the sofa and stayed there, sulking, until Gran tempted her out with a handful of bone-shaped biscuits, the ones that Megan always gave her. Even those just made her miss Megan more. Gran took her back into the kitchen away from Sid and tried to make a big fuss of her, but Ellie didn't really want to play. She was too confused.

Perhaps Megan would come and get her soon? She had been here with Megan before, after all. And she definitely remembered Sid, and the way this house smelled so strongly of cat. Megan must be coming later, Ellie decided hopefully. Every time footsteps went past on the pavement outside she pricked up her ears and wagged her tail. But as the afternoon wore on, she stopped bothering. It never was Megan, and now it was getting dark.

She padded over to her basket and stared at it miserably. If Megan was coming to get her, she wouldn't need her basket. Her food bowls were here too, and her toys. Why would they be here if Megan was coming to take her home?

"Can I talk to Ellie, Gran?" Megan asked, gripping the phone tightly.

"I'm not sure that's a very good idea, Megan," Gran said gently. "It might upset her. She'll be fine. I'm going to put a hot water bottle in her basket, and she's got her blanket and all her usual things. I expect she'll have settled down by the morning."

Which means she hasn't settled down now, Megan thought unhappily as she said goodbye. Ellie was hating being at Gran's, just as Megan had thought she would.

They were having fish and chips for tea, as a treat, so they didn't have to cook, but Megan hardly ate anything.

It wasn't the same without Ellie lurking hopefully under the table in case anyone dropped a chip.

She was feeling so miserable she went to bed early, but it took her ages to get to sleep – her room was full of boxes, and they all looked strange and gloomy in the dark. *Only till Tuesday*, Megan told herself. *Today's Sunday. Tuesday afternoon, I'll have Ellie back.*

That night, Ellie was left alone in Gran's kitchen. She had her own familiar basket and her blanket, which was wrapped round a cosy hot water bottle, but she was still desperately homesick.

She whined unhappily for a long while, but Gran didn't come down. Ellie was tired, but her basket felt wrong with the hot water bottle in it. It had cooled down now, and it sloshed and wobbled when she moved. Ellie tried to scrabble it out, but it was heavy, so she picked it up in her teeth and dragged it instead. Still it wouldn't budge. She tugged again and the water started to leak out over her blanket.

Ellie howled. Why had Megan abandoned her?

Chapter Four

Ellie woke up in her damp basket. She eyed the hot water bottle worriedly. People didn't like it when she chewed things. She looked up anxiously as the kitchen door opened, wondering if Gran would be very cross.

But she only laughed. "Oh dear, they did say you liked chewing things at the moment. It's all right, Ellie, I know you didn't mean to be naughty. It was probably silly of me to let you have it. I just didn't think. Don't be sad, little one, you'll see Megan again soon."

Ellie stared up at Gran with mournful eyes, as she tidied up her damp things. Even though Gran was being friendly, she didn't want to stay here. If only she could go back home to Megan.

Ellie was good at finding things, and she was best at finding Megan. She smelled special, and Ellie could always find her. She knew when Megan was coming home from school – she could just feel it. She somehow knew when it was time to go and sit by the door, so she could be there to see Megan as soon as she got inside.

So it would be no problem to find Megan, Ellie was sure. But finding her meant she had to get out first, and she wasn't at all sure about that.

Gran fed Ellie, then let Sid into the kitchen to give him breakfast. After that, she left the door open so Ellie could get out of the kitchen too. Gran watched them anxiously, but this time the cat and the puppy stayed out of each other's way.

After a while, Ellie crept out of the kitchen, watching carefully for Sid. She was fairly sure he was in his favourite place – on the back of the sofa, so he could look out of the window and see exactly what was going on in the street.

The front door was very big and very solid. It had a handle, which Ellie couldn't reach, even standing on her hind legs. The letter box was at the bottom of the door, but even though she could get her claws into it to scratch it open, it was only big enough for her nose and even that hurt. Ellie sat staring at the door hopelessly, then she gave her ears a determined shake. If she couldn't open it, she would just have to wait until someone opened it for her.

She hung around the hallway all morning, waiting for the door to be opened and half-playing with her squeaky fish toy.

She was just scrambling underneath a chest of drawers, trying to reach the squeaky fish, when there was the shrill sound of the doorbell. Ellie jumped, banging her head on the bottom of the chest.

She could hear someone shifting around on the doorstep. This was her chance!

Ellie wriggled herself round under the chest, so that her nose was sticking out, and watched as Gran hurried to answer the door. It was the postman with a parcel. Gran opened the door wider to take the sheet of paper she needed to sign, and Ellie's ears pricked up as she saw what was beyond it. Gran's didn't have a fenced-in front garden like Megan's house did, just a flower bed and then straight on to the pavement. As Gran turned away from the door to rest the sheet of paper on the very chest Ellie was hiding under, Ellie darted out of the door.

Ellie's heart was thumping as she hid herself behind an enormous clump of stripy leaves under the front window. She had expected the postman to see her and shout, and maybe try to catch her, but he was too busy chatting away with Gran. Still, Ellie was sure Gran would see her if she tried to run down the street now. Hiding was best. She watched anxiously as Gran gave the sheet back, and the door began to close. Was she going to notice?

Some strange sense made her look up just then, and she nearly gave herself away with a yelp.

Sid was staring down at her from his perch on the back of the sofa. He knew she was there. What if he mewed and Gran discovered she'd got out?

Ellie watched Sid nervously. Should she run now, and see if she could get far enough away in the few seconds she had left? But Sid wasn't meowing to get Gran's attention. He was sitting very still, just watching with disapproving eyes, the tip of his tail twitching very slightly.

The front door slammed shut. Ellie gulped. *He wasn't going to stop her.*

She supposed it made sense. He didn't want her in his house any more than she wanted to be there. Ellie wagged her tail at him gratefully, and sneaked out from behind the bush and on to the pavement.

She needed to get away from Gran's house fast, before Gran realized what had happened and came to find her. Ellie looked around, her tail wagging very slightly. She couldn't help but be excited. She was heading back to Megan! She was going to find her, all by herself!

She was going home.

Ellie skittered quickly across the road, making for a little lane with high hedges that led down between some of the houses. She'd be out of sight from Gran's house quickly here, she was sure.

Once she was in
the lane she raced as
fast as she could.
They had gone
down here on the
walk yesterday; it
was brambly and
overgrown, with lots
of hiding places.

Finally she ran out of breath and
collapsed, panting, underneath a
tangle of brambles. She lay in the leafy
dimness, breathing fast, and loving the
feeling of being out on her own. Walks
with Megan were the best thing, of
course, but it was fun not to have a lead
on and to be able to go where she
liked. The bramble bush smelled nice.
Earthy, but sweet at the same time.

Ellie tried to work out which way she should go next. Where was Megan? Which way?

She rested her nose on her paws. It wasn't that she was going to sniff Megan out exactly, that would be silly, she was much too far away for that. This was different from finding Megan's scent. It was more of a feel. Megan – and home – was that way.

Ellie wriggled eagerly out from under the brambles and set off down the lane. She knew it was going to be a long way – longer than any walk she'd done before – but she wasn't scared. She was Megan's dog, not Gran's, and she was meant to be with Megan.

Back at the house, Gran was searching anxiously for Ellie. She hadn't missed her until a few minutes ago, when she had put out Ellie's lunch, and she was hoping that the puppy was hiding in the house somewhere.

"Ellie! Ellie! Here, girl! Where are you?"

Gran crouched down to check behind the sofa, in case Sid had frightened her again. The cat was still curled up on the back of the sofa.

"Where can she be, Sid?" Gran muttered worriedly. "Oh, she can't have got out when the postman came? I would have seen her, surely. And that's the only time I've opened the door. But then where is she? I've looked everywhere."

Gran thought sadly of Megan – they'd be leaving their old house about now, she expected. Megan would be so excited; how could she spoil their moving day by telling them Ellie was lost? But if she didn't find the little dog soon, she would have to.

Sid followed as she went out into the hallway and opened the front door. Gran looked anxiously up and down the street, while Sid coiled round her ankles, purring lovingly.

He really didn't like dogs in his house.

The lane led out on to a main road. It was a busy road, and it didn't have wide pavements for people and dogs to walk on, like the ones Ellie was used to. She stood hesitating on the little patch of ground where the lane and the road met, and watched the cars whooshing past. She wasn't supposed to go near cars. She had been very carefully trained to sit and wait at the edge of thc pavement until Megan said to walk.

Cautiously, Ellie stretched out one paw on to the road, then jumped back with a frightened yelp as a car shot by in a speeding rush of air. Ellie looked around and decided that she wouldn't cross, even though the lane went on over the other side of the road. She would walk along the edge of the road instead. She was fairly sure she would still be going the right way. She set off, but the edge of the road was only a narrow fringe of dusty grass below the hedges. Every time a car went past it ruffled Ellie's fur, and the tyres screeched and scared her. She kept jumping into the hedge in fright.

Ellie was cowering in the hedge waiting for an enormous lorry to thunder past, when she realized that just in front of her was a hole. It was a gap in the thick hedge, leading away from this horrible, frightening road! Ellie darted through it and found herself in a field. This was much better.

There were no cars, only long grass that was fun to run through. Ellie darted across the field happily. This was much the best way to go – no more roads, she decided, at least until she got close to Megan's house, where there were roads all around.

Ellie reached the hedge to the next field and nosed along it, looking for a good place to scramble through. It was thick and prickly, but suddenly she found a small tunnel. Ellie wriggled into it – then stopped.

She was stuck! Her collar had caught on something. She pulled frantically, but the collar only tightened around her neck until it hurt. She tried again, and again, but she couldn't break the collar, or the branch it had caught on.

At last, worn out from pulling, she sat still, whimpering a little. Something else must use this tunnel, and she didn't want to be here when it came back. Pulling at the collar just wasn't going to work – but when Megan had first put it on her, she had managed to get it off, hadn't she? It had been a little big and it wasn't now, but surely if she really tried? Instead of pulling forwards, Ellie wriggled backwards, twisting her neck so that she reversed out of her collar, wrenching it over her ears.

Ellie fell backwards, rolling over in the leaves. She had done it! Her ears felt like she had half pulled them off, but although her collar was still stuck in the hedge, she wasn't. Ellie stepped out into the next field, her legs shaky with relief.

The next hedge was easy; she edged through it on her tummy and hardly even caught her fur. But as she wriggled through she could smell something strange on the other side… The field she came out in was full of cows. Ellie had only ever seen cows at a distance, and she'd never walked through a field full of them. They were very large. She stood watching for a moment, but the cows didn't seem to notice her. Most of them were grazing, though a few were lying down quietly.

She took a cautious step out into the field, then started to trot quickly across it, keeping herself low to the ground and hoping the cows wouldn't notice her. The problem was that they were scattered everywhere, so she had to go close to a few of them. Luckily, she scampered past so quickly that they hardly had time to turn their huge heads before she'd left them behind. But a few of them got nervously to their feet at the sight of the dog.

Ellie was nearly at the far hedge when she heard a heavy, lumbering tread behind her. She darted a look over her shoulder, her heart suddenly racing at double speed. An enormous black-and-white cow was thundering towards her, head lowered to show off short but business-like horns. It was staring angrily straight at Ellie, and it snorted at her in fury.

Ellie ran faster than she ever had before, racing at top speed for the hedge. She could feel the cow's hot breath as it huffed and blew behind her. Its enormous hooves trampled the grass, inches away from her tail. Ellie let out a frightened bark. She had to go faster!

Chapter Five

Megan stood in her bedroom, surrounded by boxes. It felt so strange that she had been doing just the same thing a couple of hours ago, but in her old house. There her room had looked really sad, like the end of something, but here it was a new start. It was so exciting! She just wished she had Ellie here to see everything too. She peered out of her window at the big garden, sloping down to a stream, and the woods on the other side. Tomorrow she could go and explore it all with Ellie!

Megan was suddenly desperate to talk to Gran and find out if Ellie was OK. She hurried downstairs.

"Dad, can I borrow your mobile?" Megan asked, bursting into the kitchen.

But Dad was already on the phone, looking anxious.

Megan made a "sorry!" face, but Dad only smiled at her distractedly.

"What's the matter?" Megan asked. Even the air in the kitchen felt full of worry.

"It's Gran on the phone," Mum said quietly, putting her arm around Megan. "She called to say that she thinks Ellie slipped out of the door this morning. But she's sure Ellie can't have got far."

"But, but – where can she have gone?" Megan asked, in a frightened whisper. "She hardly knows anywhere round there. She'll get lost!"

Megan sat down at the table, feeling sick. She would never have let Ellie go if she'd thought this might happen. How could Gran have let her get out?

Dad ended the call, then sat down next to her and covered her hand with his. "Gran's going to come round and pick you up so you can go and look for Ellie with her."

Megan nodded, feeling a little bit better. But it was so hard to think of Ellie, lost and lonely and scared. She had to try very hard not to cry.

Gran hugged her when she arrived, and she looked so upset that Megan forgot to be cross and just hugged her back.

"We'll find her, Megan," she promised. "I'm so sorry. She must have slipped out when the postman came.

I just didn't see. She's probably gone off exploring in the woods. The moment she hears your voice, she's sure to come running."

They drove back to Gran's, and then set off into the woods that ran behind the cottages, calling and calling.

But Ellie didn't come running, as Megan had so hoped she would. The daffodils were flowering and it was so beautiful – Megan had been looking forward to walking here with her dog so much. But all she could think about now was how scared Ellie would be out here on her own. She was still so little, and most of their walks were in the park. Ellie could get trapped in a rabbit hole, or fall in a stream! Megan sniffed hard, and rubbed her sleeve across her eyes.

"Let's go and try down the lane," Gran suggested, looking around one last time. "I just don't think she can be here, she would have heard us calling."

They found no sign of Ellie in the lane either. They went all the way down to the road, and Megan watched the cars speeding by. What if Ellie had been run over? She had tried so hard to teach her to be careful, but she was only a puppy, and she might easily have run into the road.

"I don't think she'd come along here," Gran said, hugging her. "Don't worry, Megan. Look, Ellie would be frightened of those cars if she was on her own. She wouldn't try to cross. Come on, we'll go back home. I've already asked my neighbours, but we'll go and ask round the village if anyone's seen her. Someone's sure to have done."

But Gran looked worried. It was as though Ellie had simply disappeared.

Ellie made a big leap and shot into the hedge, the cow snorting angrily behind her. It lowered its horns, as Ellie fought and scrambled her way through the twigs. She gave a yelp of relief as she struggled out into tufts of long grass on the other side of the hedge.

The cow snorted grumpily and lumbered away, and Ellie collapsed panting on the soft grass. She'd left her collar in the last hedge, but it felt like she'd left half her fur in this one.

Now that she was safely away from the cows, Ellie realized how hungry she was, and thirsty too. She hadn't had lunch, and it felt a long way past lunchtime now. But although the sun was sinking, it was still warm. The air felt sticky, and black clouds were gathering behind the trees.

The quiet lane was leading to houses, just a few, but there might be some food around, Ellie thought hopefully. And somewhere to rest. She didn't want to stay out in the open all night. She didn't like that strange close feeling in the air. It made her fur feel prickly.

"Mum rang the police just now and reported her missing." Megan gulped. "She's been gone all day, Bella! The policeman said it's good that she's microchipped, because if someone brings her in, they can check. Mum gave them the new address. Gran and I searched and searched, and then we made posters on her computer. We've stuck them up everywhere, but no one's called. I wish you were here to help us look." Megan was sitting in her new bedroom, borrowing Dad's mobile to call Bella. She hated having to tell her that Ellie was missing. It made it seem even more real.

"Oh, Megan!" Bella sounded almost as upset as she was. "Have you been all through those woods you told me about?"

"We've searched the woods twice, and Mum says I can't go again now, it's getting dark," Megan said sadly. "I just want her back. She'll be so scared, Bella. I hate thinking of her all on her own."

The first house Ellie came to kept its bins tightly closed. She headed on past. There was a good smell coming from somewhere close. Bread, she thought, sneaking carefully down the side of a house and squirming under an iron gate. Yes! Bread crusts, scattered all over a patio around a bird table. Ellie gobbled them greedily. She was so glad to find some food that she didn't notice she was being watched. The slam of a door made her jump back in fright. An elderly lady came out, looking cross and waving a broom. She poked it at Ellie, who skittered back in horror.

"Shoo! Out of here, bad dog! Don't you scare away my birds! Shoo! Go home!" And she banged the brush on the paving stones, making Ellie squeak with fright. The puppy shot across the garden towards the gap under the gate, wriggling out and away as quickly as she could.

Once she was safely a few houses away, she hid under a car, shivering. She hadn't known the bread was special; she was only hungry. Ellie whimpered. She wanted Megan back. Then she shook her ears determinedly. She was on her way to Megan. She had a feeling that she had walked along this lane before, with Megan and Gran when they were out together. It was definitely on the way home. She poked out her nose from under the car, checking for the old lady, but there was no one around.

It was getting dark, though. She wanted to keep going, but the stormy feeling in the air was getting stronger, and she could hear low growls of thunder. It made the fur stand up on her back. She would have to find somewhere to stop for the night. All of a sudden, the greyish sky split with a bright flash of lightning, and a heartbeat later thunder crashed down. Ellie howled, and dived through a garden gate.

She raced into the garden, looking round desperately for somewhere to hide from those horrible noises. A house! A little wooden house, just here in the corner, just the right size for a dog. There were spotted curtains blowing in the window, and the door was open the tiniest crack. Ellie nosed at it, pushing it wider, and sneaked inside. There was even a cushion on the floor, along with a scatter of crayons. Ellie collapsed on to it gratefully and closed her eyes. It seemed a very long time since she'd run away that morning.

Soon Ellie was fast asleep.

A few miles away, Megan was lying awake. She wasn't really scared of thunder, not when she was safe inside. But tonight it was terrifying. She kept imagining Ellie outside, frightened by the growling thunder. What if she was hurt? What if she was hiding under a tree to get out of the rain, and the tree was struck by lightning?

Megan watched the rain beating against the windows, and shivered. It was a long time before she finally huddled under her bedclothes and drifted off into a troubled sleep.

The creak of the wooden door opening woke Ellie with a start. She shot upright, backing nervously into the corner of the playhouse.

A little boy was staring at her. He looked just as amazed as she did.

"A dog!" he breathed delightedly. "A dog's come!"

He sounded friendly, and Ellie relaxed a little, but she didn't go closer. Most children she met with Megan loved her and wanted to stroke her, but Megan wouldn't let her jump up at children, or even sniff them. One little girl had seen her walking past, and then Ellie had gone to sniff her hand, and she'd squealed. Ellie had felt quite hurt. So now she watched this little boy carefully.

"Hello, dog…" He was crouching down now, staring into her eyes, and Ellie was sure that this one wasn't going to cry. "I'm William. Have you come to stay? Are you going to live in my house?" He sounded very excited. "I know! You're hungry! Grandad's dog is always hungry." He leaned closer, and whispered, "Mummy's on the phone. I was having breakfast, but I came out when she wasn't looking. You can have my breakfast." He scrambled out of the little house and dashed away.

Ellie stood there blinking, not quite sure what was going on. She pattered over to the door, and peered out. William was coming back, more slowly now, his dark head bent earnestly over a bowl, with something balanced on the edge of it.

"There! My Weetabix. I've already had two, so you can have that one. And this is a bacon sandwich. I don't like bacon anyway."

Ellie could smell the bacon. After nothing but stale bread crusts since yesterday, it smelt like heaven. She trotted over to him and took it delicately from his hand as he held it out to her. It disappeared in about three bites.

"Wow, you are hungry." William sounded impressed.

Ellie sighed with pleasure, licking the bacon from round her whiskers, and looked hopefully at the bowl.

"Oh! Do you like Weetabix too?" He put the bowl down on the ground for her and watched hopefully.

Ellie sniffed at it with interest. Oh, yes, she recognized this. She had proper dog food at home now, but when she'd been very small she'd had this too, for breakfast. She liked it. She gulped it down, licking the bowl out thoroughly, then sat down, scratching her ear with one hind paw. She always did that after meals. It felt good.

William laughed. "Funny dog," he said, crouching down to stroke her gently.

Ellie closed her eyes, and leaned against him happily. He reminded her of Megan, even though he was so little. She would see Megan soon, she thought excitedly.

"Oh!" William straightened up. "Mum's calling me. I have to go.

I'm going to ask her if you can stay! Mum! Mum!" He dashed back to the house, and Ellie watched the kitchen door swing shut behind him. She would have liked to stay with him for longer, but she was sure she wasn't that far from home now.

She crept past the playhouse and back under the garden gate. She paused for a moment outside William's house, to give him one last grateful bark, then she went on her way.

Chapter Six

A few hours later, Ellie stood looking down into the river. She was sure she had just seen a fish. She had been here once before, one wonderful afternoon when they'd had a picnic, and Mum had told Megan off for feeding her bits of sausage roll. Remembering it made her feel hungry. She had walked a very long way since the bacon sandwich.

Ellie set off again along the riverbank, wondering if she could catch a fish. That one had looked very slippery. And although she loved getting wet, she hadn't had a lot of practice at swimming.

Ah. Maybe this would be better than a fish. Just ahead of her, standing on the riverbank, was a man with a fishing rod, staring out over the water at his float. But what really interested Ellie was his bag of sandwiches, lying by his tackle box.

Ellie sneaked closer, and then darted out from behind a tree and seized a sandwich.

"Hey!" The fisherman shouted crossly, but he couldn't chase her without getting tangled in his line. He was trying to lay it down carefully, but Ellie didn't wait for him. Gripping the sandwich in her teeth, she ran for it, racing away down the overgrown path.

When his shouts died away into the distance, Ellie sat down to eat her prize: a tuna sandwich. So she was having fish after all!

She licked up the last crumbs from the grass and sighed happily. She felt much better now. She stood up and gave herself a brisk shake. It was time to set off home again.

"Hello? Yes, this is Lindsey. Oh!" Mum beckoned frantically to Megan, who was listlessly picking at her tea. She just didn't feel like eating – it made her worry about how hungry Ellie must be, after a day and a half with no food.

"Who is it?" she asked, staring at Mum's excited face. Then she sat up straight, gasping. "Is it the posters? Has someone seen her?"

Mum was nodding. "Yes, yes, a Labrador puppy. Yes, quite small. Let me write that down. By the bridge. Oh dear, I am sorry. And that was this morning? Oh, thank you so much for calling us. Yes, I hope we will too." She ended the call, and turned to

Megan, who was now standing right next to her, trying desperately to hear what the person on the other end of the line had been saying. "That was a man from the village who was fishing down by Selby Bridge this morning. Ellie stole his sandwiches!" Mum hugged her, laughing.

Megan smiled. "I was just thinking about how hungry she must be!"

"Come on, call your dad. Let's go and look for her. It's getting dark, but we should be able to see for a while."

Ellie's paws were aching, but she felt so proud of herself. She had done it. She could see Megan's school playground, and the park was just round the next corner. She was so close! Despite her weariness, she trotted along faster. In a few minutes she would be back with Megan. She was just in time – already it was starting to get dark.

This was her road, and there was her house! Ellie looked carefully up and down the road for cars, then crossed over to her own front gate. She couldn't open it, but it was a pretty iron one that she could slip through, even though it was a tight fit. She stood outside the front door and barked happily. They were going to be so pleased to see her!

No one came to the door, so she scratched at it with her front paws and barked again, louder and louder.

At last she heard
footsteps. Ellie
barked and jumped
delightedly. She was
going to see Megan!
But when the door
opened, it wasn't
Megan. Or even her
mum or dad. There
was a strange woman
standing there,
looking down
at her in
surprise.

Ellie whimpered, tucking her tail between her legs in confusion.

Megan had gone. She had left, and abandoned Ellie with Gran. Megan didn't want her any more.

"What's going on?" A man was coming down the hall now, looking surprised. "Oh! A dog? Has it got a collar?"

"No, I don't think so." The woman bent down to look.

Ellie backed away from the doorstep, miserably. She didn't know what to do. But the woman who'd answered the door followed her, talking gently. "Don't be scared, puppy, are you lost? Oh, look, she's shivering, poor little thing. She's so pretty, and she can't be very old."

The man came out too. "She must have slipped out of someone's house, don't you think? Maybe we'd better keep her for the night. We'll have to put her in the shed, though. Jasper would go crazy if we brought another dog in, and he's already upset about the new house. We can take her round to the police station in the morning, and see if she's been microchipped." And he reached down and scooped Ellie up.

The man carried Ellie round the side of her house, only it wasn't her house any more, and she wasn't even allowed in. They put down a rug for her in the shed, with a bowl of water and some dog biscuits. It was comfortable, but she was in the garden and she was shut up, when she should be inside, upstairs sleeping on Megan's bed.

Her family had gone away and left her. She just didn't understand. Even though Megan's dad had been cross with her, Megan had still cuddled her and talked to her and loved her the same way, hadn't she? Why had Megan left her behind? Had she just forgotten her?

Ellie buried her nose under her paws and whimpered. She'd spent so long trying to get home, and now home wasn't there.

Chapter Seven

Megan woke up and lay staring at the ceiling for a second. It looked wrong. Then she remembered she was in her new house. She felt a rush of excitement, until she looked down at the empty space at the end of her bed and remembered that Ellie was missing. She wished she could just go back to sleep and this would only be a dream.

She had been so hopeful yesterday evening when they'd got the phone call. They'd driven straight down to Selby Bridge, which was on the way back to their old house. It was a beautiful place, and they'd taken Ellie there before for walks. She and Mum and Dad had searched all the way along the riverbank, calling, and banging Ellie's food bowl, something suggested by the friendly policeman that Mum had spoken to on the phone yesterday.

At last Dad had taken her hand. "Megan, it's getting dark. I think we have to stop."

"But we can't! She was here!" Megan had protested.

"We can come back in the morning and look again," Mum promised.

So Megan had to get up now. That man had definitely seen Ellie – there couldn't be two lost Labrador puppies, could there? She climbed out of bed wearily. She felt like she'd been dreaming about Ellie all night. In the worst dream, the puppy had been in the middle of a road, and Megan could hear a car coming. She shivered.

Megan started to pull on her dressing gown, then suddenly she stopped and sat down on her bed again, staring wide-eyed at the photo on the shelf. It was a picture of her and Bella and Ellie playing in their old garden. She reached over and picked it up. How could she have been so stupid? Ellie had been at Selby Bridge. Halfway back to their old house!

Ellie wasn't lost at all. She was trying to go home!

"Mum! Dad!" Megan went racing into their room. "Dad, where's your mobile, we have to call the people at our old house. Ellie's gone home!"

Her parents were still half asleep, and her dad blinked at her wearily. "What do you mean?"

Megan sat down on the edge of the bed and started to explain. "She was really upset about being at Gran's, wasn't she. She didn't understand what was going on. She doesn't know we've moved, Dad! She's trying to get back to our old house! She'd got halfway yesterday morning. She's probably home by now!" Megan suddenly frowned. "Oh, no. She's going to find somebody else in our house." Her voice shook.

Mum sat up. "Megan, I don't think Ellie can have got that far. How could she find the way? It's a lovely idea, but..."

"She got as far as Selby Bridge!" Megan pointed out.

"Yes, I suppose so..."

"You do hear of dogs doing that kind of thing," Dad put in thoughtfully. "Maybe we should ring the house, just in case. But it's too early right now."

Mum and Dad made her wait a whole hour before they called. Megan had walked in circles around the kitchen; she couldn't face breakfast. Now she was pressed close to Dad, trying to hear the phone conversation.

"She came to the door? Last night? No, we hadn't thought of calling you before, it's such a long way, you see. Nearly ten miles! That's wonderful. Yes, yes, of course, I see. I'm sure she would be fine in the shed. Yes, we'll come straight away. We'll see you soon."

"They've found her! They really have! Oh, Dad!" Megan was dancing now, jumping and flinging herself at her parents to hug them. Then she raced to get her boots on. They were going to get Ellie back!

Ellie lay on the rug in the chilly shed, wondering where she should go, now that she didn't have a home any more.

She didn't want to go back to Gran's. Sid didn't like her, and she didn't want to live with him. She would have to find somewhere new.

The problem was, Ellie didn't want anywhere new. She only wanted Megan. But she certainly couldn't stay here. Ellie scrambled over the tangle of old garden equipment that was still cluttering up the shed, sniffing out that fresh, cold breeze. There was a loose board in the wall! Ellie pushed it to one side and started to wriggle through. Her fur felt full of dust and splinters. She squeezed out the other side and shook herself briskly.

The new people had left the side gate open, and Ellie raced out down the side of the house. She didn't want them to shut her up again. She was about to run straight out of the front gate, but something stopped her.

Lying on the path, half-hidden by the bins, was one of her toys. Her favourite toy. The red-and-white-striped knotted rope toy that Bella had given her. Ellie picked it up in her teeth and shook it happily. It was so good to chew, and she loved it when Megan pulled the other end and then they'd play tug-of-war together.

Madly shaking the toy from side to side, Ellie knew, with sudden, happy certainty, that Megan had not left her behind. Not on purpose. Megan loved to play with her, and stroke her, and talk to her.

Ellie trotted determinedly out of her

old front garden, squeezing quickly through the front gate, and set off down the street. She wasn't sure where she was going, but she was not going to give up. She reached the end of the road and looked around thoughtfully. She usually walked down here with Megan to pick up Bella on her way to school.

Bella! Bella loved her, and she loved Megan. Bella would know where Megan was! Ellie raced down the road, yelping with excitement, still carrying the rope toy.

As she turned the corner, she didn't

notice a familiar car driving down the road. The car pulled up outside the house and Megan leaped out. Without waiting for her parents, she went running up the garden path of their old house, and rang and rang on the doorbell.

Chapter Eight

Outside Bella's front gate, Ellie dropped the rope toy, and sat down neatly, just like she always used to. Then she barked loudly, three times.

She waited. She was just about to bark again, when Bella's front door opened, and Bella rushed out on to the path.

"Ellie! I thought it was you barking, but Mum said it couldn't possibly be!

What are you doing here? Megan said on the phone last night someone had seen you at Selby Bridge. How did you get all the way back here?" Bella flung open the gate. "Oh, Ellie, we've all been so worried about you! Come on, Ellie, come! Here, girl!"

Bella held open the gate and beckoned Ellie in.

Ellie picked up her toy and followed her. She trusted Bella not to shut her in a shed. Bella would help her get back to Megan, she was sure.

"Mum, Mum, look! Ellie's here! It was her barking, I told you!" Bella and Ellie dashed down the hall to Bella's mum in the kitchen. "I have to call Megan, please, Mum?"

"Has she come all the way from

Woodlands Cottage? She can't have done, it must be at least ten miles." Bella's mum was staring at Ellie in amazement. "She doesn't have a collar, are you sure this is Ellie? You haven't just stolen someone's dog?"

"Mu-um! Of course it's Ellie! Look, she's carrying the toy that I bought her for Christmas. Besides, only Ellie would know to sit at the gate and bark three times. Oh, they're not answering." Bella put down the phone with a crash and stared at Ellie. "Is it really ten miles? How could she walk that far? And how did she know the way?"

"Well, dogs can be very clever," her mum said doubtfully. "But I don't know, to be honest. Because she was so desperate to find Megan, I suppose."

Ellie barked, her eyes wide with hope. *Megan!* They had definitely said Megan.

"She heard you say it." Bella laughed. "Are you trying to find Megan, Ellie?"

Ellie jumped up with her paws on Bella's knees, and barked and barked, wagging her tail frantically.

"It's OK, Megan will be here soon, I promise. She'll come and get you. Or we could take her to Megan's new house, couldn't we, Mum?"

Her mum frowned. "That might not be a good idea. She could get upset. Why don't we try ringing the house again?"

Bella nodded. "I have missed you, Ellie. But not as much as Megan has.

She's been searching for you all over the place." She stroked Ellie's soft head. "She's going to be so happy to have you back."

Megan sat in the car outside her old house, gulping back tears. Her mum was sitting next to her, trying to calm her down, and her dad was leaning over from the front seat.

"I know it's hard, Megan, but I promise we'll find her. Come on, this is good news. We know she was here last night! That's a really good start."

Megan nodded, but she couldn't stop crying. "She came all this way to find us," she whispered tearfully. "And then there was someone else in her house. Another dog as well! She must have thought we just didn't love her any more. What if she's gone off to find somewhere else to live?"

"I'm sure she won't have," Mum said firmly. "Ellie won't give up. She made it this far, didn't she? She'll be around here somewhere, probably just a bit confused. Let's go and try the park."

But Ellie wasn't in the park, or in any of the streets around their old house. They called, Megan's dad whistled, and they stopped to ask everyone they saw. But there was no trace of her.

"She's gone." Megan had stopped crying now. She was almost too upset to cry. "We had our chance and now we've lost her for ever."

"Megan!" Her mum crouched down and hugged her. "I never thought I'd hear you giving up. You have to keep going – Ellie needs you to find her."

Megan nodded, biting her lip. Her mum was right. Ellie wouldn't give up on her, would she? "Can we go and see Bella? Get her to look out for Ellie? She won't know Ellie's back here, and she could ask people from school if she sees them."

"Good idea," her mum said. "Let's go back to the car – we'll drive round."

Megan rang Bella's doorbell, thinking back to the last time she'd done that – on the final day of school, when Bella had been running so late she hadn't come out of the house when Ellie barked.

She'd been pulling on her coat when she opened the door, and she'd had a piece of toast sticking out of her mouth. She'd fed a little bit of it to Ellie.

Megan blinked. Why was there barking coming from inside Bella's house? She didn't have a dog…

Just then, the door flew open. "I knew it! Did you get my message? I've called about six times! Why didn't you call me back?" Bella's words were falling over each other in excitement, but Megan hardly heard her.

She was hugging Ellie – Ellie who'd leaped into her arms as soon as Bella opened the door. The puppy's paws were on Megan's shoulders in a golden furry hug, and she was licking Megan's face all over.

Megan's parents laughed delightedly, and Bella's mum started telling them about Ellie's sudden appearance.

Megan beamed at Bella. "We didn't get any message, we weren't at home, you see. The people from the new house had found Ellie, but she slipped out of the shed. They had to put her in there because they had a dog too, so – urrgh, Ellie, don't lick my mouth!

So they shut Ellie in, but there's a hole in the shed wall, so she got out. She must have decided to come to you, she knows you really love her. Bella, you found her!" And she hugged Bella too, squidging Ellie in between them.

"No, she found me," Bella giggled. "She turned up and barked outside the gate. I thought I was dreaming!"

"Oh, Ellie, I'm never letting you go anywhere again," Megan gasped in between licks. "You're such a clever, brilliant dog – how did you find your way back here?"

Ellie sighed deeply, and laid her chin on Megan's shoulder. All of a sudden, she felt very, very tired.

It had been a long journey, but now, at last, she was back home with Megan.

Out Now:

Out Now:

HOLLY WEBB

Holly Webb started out as a children's book editor, and wrote her first series for the publisher she worked for. She has been writing ever since, with over one hundred books to her name. Holly lives in Berkshire, with her husband and three young sons. Holly's pet cats are always nosying around when she is trying to type on her laptop.

For more information
about Holly Webb visit:

www.holly-webb.com